MOG'S
Bad Thing

written and illustrated by

Judith Kerr

HarperCollins *Children's Books*

For Tom
with all my love

Picture books by Judith Kerr

Mog the Forgetful Cat*
Mog's Christmas*
Mog and the Baby*
Mog in the Dark
Mog's Amazing Birthday Caper
Mog and Bunny
Mog and Barnaby
Mog on Fox Night
Mog and the Granny
Mog and the V.E.T.*
Mog's Bad Thing*
Goodbye Mog
How Mrs Monkey Missed the Ark
When Willy Went to the Wedding
Birdie Halleluyah!
The Other Goose
Goose in a Hole
Twinkles, Arthur and Puss*
One Night in the Zoo*
My Henry
The Great Granny Gang
*also available on audio CD

First published in hardback in Great Britain by HarperCollins Publishers Ltd in 2000. First published in paperback by Picture Lions in 2001.
This edition published by HarperCollins Children's Books in 2005

25
ISBN: 978 0 00 664755 3

Picture Lions and Collins Picture Books are imprints of HarperCollins Publishers Ltd. HarperCollins Children's Books is a division of HarperCollins Publishers Ltd. A CIP catalogue record for this title is available from the British Library.

Visit our website at: www.harpercollins.co.uk

Printed in China

One day Mog was coming home to her garden.
She had been on a mouse hunt all night
and she was very tired.
Mog thought, "I need a big sleep."

But first she went round her garden
to see if it was just as she'd left it.
The grass was still there.

The flowers were still there.

The tree was still there, and so
was her lavatory behind the tree.
Mog thought, "That's all right then."

It was starting to rain, so she went
into the house.

Mr Bunce from the pet shop was there with Mr Thomas.
He said, “Hullo Mog. All ready for the cat show tomorrow?”
Debbie said, “There’s going to be a cat show in our garden,
Mog, and you can be in it.”
“What if it rains?” said Nicky. “All the cats will get wet.”
“No,” said Mr Bunce, “because I’m going to put up a big tent
and the cat show will be inside it.”

Debbie said, "Perhaps Mog will win a prize."
Mr Thomas looked at Mog and Mog looked back at him.
He said, "Well... well, you never know."

Mog had her breakfast and went to have her big sleep. It was a very big sleep. It was so big that she only woke up after everyone else had gone to bed. Mog thought, “Now for another mouse hunt.”

But when she looked out she had a terrible shock. Her garden had disappeared. The grass had disappeared. The flowers had disappeared. The tree had disappeared and, worst of all, so had her lavatory behind the tree.

Instead, there in the dark was a big white flappy-floppy thing.
The flappy-floppy thing moved in the wind. It went
flap! flap! flap! It went flap! flap! flap! with a loud
flappy noise. Mog thought, "I'd better run."
Then she thought, "But I want my lavatory."
Suddenly the flappy-floppy thing flapped right at her.
It nearly caught her nose. Mog ran.

She ran back into her house.

She ran through all
the rooms in case the
flappy-floppy thing
was coming after her.

She thought, "What shall I do?

What shall I do?"

And then Mog did a bad thing.
She did not mean to do it, but she did it.
She did it in Mr Thomas's chair.

Then she hid under the sofa where
the flappy-floppy thing couldn't
get her. She was too upset to
think any more, so she went
back to sleep.

She woke up in the morning to a great noise.
It was a shouting noise and Mr Thomas was doing the shouting.
He shouted, "Look what that horrible cat has done in my chair!
Where is that horrible cat? Just wait till I find her!"

Mog did not want Mr Thomas to find her.
When no one was looking she ran out from under the sofa
and out of the room and to the very top of the house.

She thought, "No one will ever find me here. I'll stay here for ever and ever and I'll never go downstairs again." She was very sad.

But downstairs they were all too busy to think about Mog. Mr Bunce had come to get ready for the cat show. He fixed a hole in the tent where rain was coming through.

Then he put out a table for the cats to sit on

and chairs for the cats' people.

Debbie said,
"It's time Mog
got ready too.
Where is she?"

No one had seen her. They all shouted, “Mog! Where are you, Mog?”

Mrs Thomas said, “Oh dear, here come
the first cats for the cat show.”

But there was no Mog. Then they looked in every place they could think of.
But still there was no Mog.

Debbie said, "But we can't start the cat show without Mog."
"Don't worry," said Mr Bunce. "I expect she'll suddenly appear and surprise us all."

There was no time to go on looking
for Mog because more cats were arriving.
There was the Siamese from round the corner
and Blackie from the High Street
and Ginger from the paper shop
and old Mr Ben's Tommy
and Fluffy who had
once bitten Mog's ear
and Oscar who ate three
tins of cat food every day,
and a whole lot of others.

They all went into the big tent. The cats looked at each other and the cats' people looked at each other and at each other's cats. There was a prize for the most unusual cat in the show and everyone wondered which cat would win.

A lot of people thought Fluffy was unusual.
"He's only unusual as an ear biter," said Nicky.

Mr Bunce went round making notes. He could not make notes about Mog because she was not there. "Wherever can she be?" said Debbie.

Mog was getting bored with her hiding place.
She thought she'd look out of the window.
The flappy-floppy thing had stopped flapping.
It did not look so bad in daylight.

And there was her tree! It was there! It was still there! Mog thought, "I could jump down on the flappy-floppy thing and into my garden." Then she thought, "But it might flap at me." Then she thought, "Shall I?"

Inside the tent, Mr Bunce had finished making notes. He said, "It's time to choose the winner of the show. We can choose Bertie who has unusual eyes, or Oscar who is unusually big, or Fluffy who is unusually furry, or Min who is unusually... well, unfurry, or Mrs Pussy

who has had a very unusual number of kittens..."
But something was wrong. Fluffy was getting wet.
It was raining on Fluffy. It was raining inside the tent.
"Oh dear," said Mr Bunce. "It's another hole in the roof.
The rain *will* come through."

But then something more
than rain came through.

It was something furry.
It was something stripy.
Nicky shouted, "It's Mog!"

"Well I never," said Mr Bunce. "And in a little dress! I thought Mog might surprise us but this beats everything." Mog tried to say something but only a very small noise came out. Meow! Then Mr Bunce said, "In this show we have seen some unusual cats, but none as unusual as Mog. She has flown through the air like a circus cat. She is an abro-cat... I mean acrobat. She has amazed us all and I think the prize for the most unusual cat should go to Mog."

Everyone clapped and cheered.

Well, almost everyone.

Mog got a very special prize and
Mr and Mrs Thomas got a certificate.

They were very proud. Mr Thomas was so proud that he was no longer cross about his chair. And when everyone had gone home Mr Bunce took his tent away again and Mog's garden reappeared.

It was all there just as before. The grass was there. The flowers were there. The tree was there, and so was her lavatory behind the tree. She was very happy.